4-6 yrs

LUCKY DUCK

Written by Ellen Weiss
Illustrated by Brian Lies

ALADDIN
New York London Toronto Sydney

For Sandy, David, and Vanessa —E. W.
For Jim and Pam Johnston —B. L.

First Aladdin edition February 2004

Text copyright © 2004 by Ellen Weiss
Illustrations copyright © 2004 by Brian Lies

ALADDIN PAPERBACKS
An imprint of Simon & Schuster Children's Publishing Division
1230 Avenue of the Americas
New York, NY 10020

READY-TO-READ is a registered trademark of Simon & Schuster.

Book design by Debra Sfetsios
The text of this book was set in Century Oldstyle.

Printed in the United States of America
2 4 6 8 10 9 7 5 3 1

LCCN 2003106064

ISBN 0-689-86029-3 (Aladdin pbk.)
ISBN 0-689-86030-7 (Aladdin Library edition)

Lucky Duck took a walk.

Lucky Duck stopped to talk.

Look out, Lucky Duck!

Lucky Duck saw a truck.

The truck was very,
very stuck.

Uh-oh, Lucky Duck!

8

Lucky Duck walked
down the street.

But he did not watch
his feet.

Good grief, Lucky Duck!

Lucky Duck went to the store.

He could not get in the door.

Oh no, Lucky Duck!

Lucky Duck went to the fair.

Fun and games were
everywhere.

Watch out, Lucky Duck!

Lucky Duck took a ride.

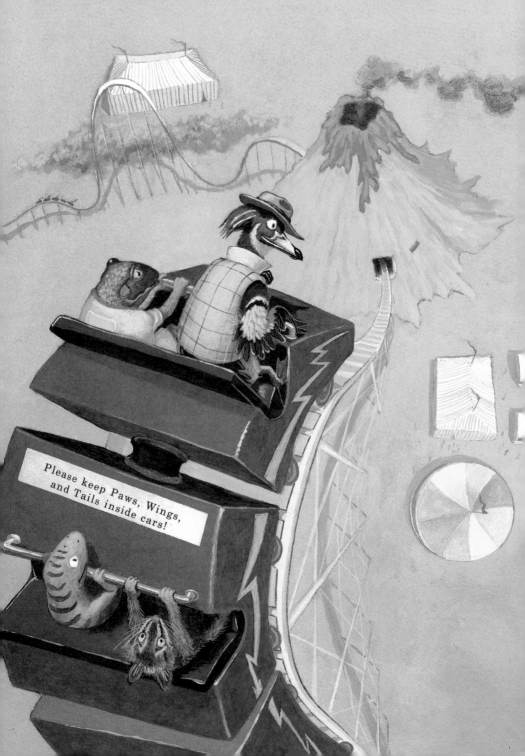

Please keep Paws, Wings, and Tails inside cars!

Lucky Duck, stay inside!

Yikes, Lucky Duck!

Lucky Duck ate some pie.

Lucky Duck,

watch that fly!

Whew, Lucky Duck!

EXIT
THANK YOU

Lucky Duck was tired,

and so—

time for Lucky Duck to go.

He smiled at everyone

he passed. . . .

And Lucky Duck was home at last.

Whoa! Watch your step, Lucky Duck!

Look out, Lucky Duck!

Hold on, Lucky Duck!

Good night, Lucky Duck!